The Mezmurs

The Mezmurs

by Melissa George

Life Rattle Press

The Mezmurs
by Melissa George

Published in Canada by Life Rattle Press, Toronto

Library and Archives Canada Cataloguing in
Publication The Mezmurs by Melissa George and
the Life Rattle Collective.

(New writers series)
Dark fantasy novella.

ISBN 978-1-987936-25-4

I. Dark fantasy novella, Canadian (English)
--Ontario --Toronto.
I. George, Melissa, 1995-, writer and editor
II. Life Rattle Collective, publisher
III. Series: New writers series

Copy Edited by Courtney Kelly

Cover Design by Marta Bielak

Dedicated to all the terrifying monsters ever created

CHAPTER I

Dear Journal

They're here.
The skittering.
Why didn't I just stay home?

Entry #1

Dear Journal,

My life has forever changed today.

I'm Shail, a ginger-bearded, husky, young Dwarf from Tinfeld. I live with my mom and dad. But my dad also works in the mines, so "living" with him is a pretty loose term. My mom runs a local general store, so she spent a lot more time than my dad raising me. When I wasn't in school, being taught about excavation, safety, or fitness, I helped my mom at the store.

Anyway, I got a job at Ebony Excavations Inc.! I was collecting the mail after dinner and there were a bunch of letters for me. I knew exactly what they were the moment I saw them. A few weeks ago, before graduating from school, I sent out applications to different mining companies. I've known for a long time that I wanted to transition from school into work right away. But now that it's happening, I'm really nervous. I wasn't sure whether I could even force myself to open the letters. But when my mom saw me staring at them, probably with a look of dread, she preached to me about how "if you don't open them then you'll regret it for the rest of your life," and stuff like that. So I tore them all open. There weren't actually all that many, but the pile seemed enormous to me. I applied to ten different mining companies around this mountain range, the Mingun Mountains, not too far so that I could still come home during the off-seasons or for vacations. My top pick was Ebony and, sure enough, they accepted me.

The letter says that I start in a week. It also has a train ticket for me. And there's a note with a list of supplies they want me to get ahead of time.

†Pickaxe
†Bedroll
†Chisel and hammer
†Rope
†Helmet
†Rations
†Uniforms
†Steel-toed boots
†Lantern

Some of this stuff I already have, like a pickaxe, lantern, and steel-toes. We needed them for school. But other things on the list, like the helmet and rations I'll need to go get. The rations will be easy, because my mom's store sells those. But the helmet will be a bit of a pain, and expensive, because it has to be fitted. I should do that tomorrow or else there won't be enough time left before I have to leave.

Just writing about the things I need to get done is stressful enough. A million questions are running through my head. Do I really want to start working? How will I get all of this in time? What happens if I don't? What if I miss my train? I'm really happy to have this job, but I'm also nervous. This will be my first time in the mines and I've never been away from home before, so what do I do if I get homesick? I guess we'll find out. One of my teachers always said we should write in journals while in the mines because it will keep us sane. Honestly, I think he should write in his own journal a little more. But I'll give it a shot. I'll try to write every day while I'm away. There can't be any harm in it, right?

It's getting late though, so I'm going to call it a night. I'll write again soon, hopefully.

Shail

CHAPTER 2

Train Ride

I'm on the train, headed to the best job ever!

Shail's boots clunked and thumped against the hardwood floorboards of the train carriage. Wooden benches jutted out from the rusty, metal walls, creating a narrow alley for one to walk up and down the car. male Dwarves of all ages lined the seats. Some of them already looked as though they had not showered in a few days. Some of them had foreign accents, which explained their uncleanliness. Clearly they came from other sides of the mountain range and had already been on the train for some time now. All of them wore the same miner's clothes as him. Shail heaved his luggage down the narrow aisle. He spotted an empty bench at the back.

On his way, he bumped the foot of a sleeping, grumpy-looking Dwarf. He began apologizing, but the man simply grunted and continued sleeping. Shail gingerly inched by the Dwarf and continued down the train car.

One man, sitting next to a window, clearly lost in thought, shook terribly. He looked mortified. As Shail passed, he noticed the man fumbling with something in his lap. It was a severely crumpled letter.

"Hey, um… Are you alright there?" Shail whispered. He stepped in-between the benches and leaned down. The man jumped and stared up at Shail. His hands fumbled with the letter. It slipped out of his grasp and hit the floor. The Dwarf made no attempt to pick it up, so Shail leant down and plucked it off the scuffed floor.

"Piece of shit, that is," the man mumbled. Shail looked at the man, bewildered, and then unfolded the letter. It looked like the one he'd received from the mining company, but this one had a large number '9' scrawled at the bottom.

"You'll be next to me," said Shail, smiling as he handed

back the letter. The man snatched the piece of parchment back. He stared down at it with disdain.

"Arsholes, all of 'em. I already did my time, ya know? Worked for 'em for almost twenty years. But now they're callin' me back. They say I didn't finish my contract, but I know I did. Just gotta be more careful this time." The Dwarf glanced back at Shail.

"They don't tell ya about the cave-ins." His eyes narrowed. "Be the first out. And don't find their den! Otherwise, they'll hunt ya down. Just stay away... Stay away from them and you'll be alright." Panic covered the man's face. Shail felt uneasy. The stranger had sweat rolling down his face now while his hands twisted and crumpled the letter. Slowly, Shail backed away. He tried to do so as subtly as possible so as not to run away from the man and seem rude. But as soon as he was out in the aisle, he couldn't help but dart away. Shail could hear the man yelling behind him,

"If ya get trapped, hole up like I did and wait out the storm!"

Shail jogged down the train. He noticed a Dwarf, young, like himself, sitting on the bench that he was heading for. The boy pressed himself against the window, gazing out and fogging the glass up with his breath. Shail wandered over, lugging his bag along. He sat down.

"Hey," Shail tucked his bag under the bench. "My name's Shail." He wiped his hand on his pants and extended it to shake. The other Dwarf turned towards Shail. The Dwarf had short, scruffy black hair and steely blue eyes. He was somewhat pudgy, definitely not like somebody ready for a labour-intensive job. The other Dwarf gave Shail's hand a weak shake. He had a slight smile on his face that didn't reach his eyes. "Is this your first time going into the mines too?" asked Shail.

"Y-yeah," the Dwarf mumbled, as he turned to look out the window again. Shail fiddled with the fringe on his shirt.

"What number did you get?" He glanced over at the other Dwarf.

"Um... e-ei-eight, I think..."

"Really?" Shail perked up. "That's great. We'll be working together." The other Dwarf seemed oblivious to Shail. "Is something wrong?"

"N-no, I'm alright." The younger Dwarf's eyebrows stitched together.

"Well, I'm nervous about leaving home for the first time," Shail said. "But I'm really excited to be going down into the mines finally. And I'm going to be working for Ebony Excavations Inc., which was my top pick." The other Dwarf stayed silent, staring out the window.

The train blew its horn and chugged out of the station. Shail glanced past the other Dwarf's head, taking in the last sight of his home. He wouldn't be back for many months.

The mid-day sun shone down on his peaceful hometown. Adults meandered along the dirt path between two rows of shops. Three children played a game of tag in farmer Turkot's beet fields. Shail couldn't see his home from the train. The house would be empty at noon anyway. He glanced over the cluster of family members waving goodbye to their loved ones on the train. Shail imagined his mother, in her pink and forest green floral frock, behind the counter at the shop. The train eased out of the station. The few faces at the station faded away.

The train ride went smoothly. Shail enjoyed watching the landscapes zoom past the window. A wide pond glistened in the sun, surrounded by tall marshy reeds. Deer darted into the dense underbrush of a pine forest. And a horse raced the train in the rain as it rattled by the muddy pasture. He had never traveled before, so the sights fascinated him. As much as Shail wished he could be having a conversation with his newfound teammate, he satisfied himself by gazing around at his surroundings. He memorized the cracks, scuffs, and scratches on the floorboards at his feet, imagining all of the other Dwarves that had sat in his spot. He analyzed the rust that seeped out wherever two pieces of metal had been welded together, and made up stories about where the other Dwarves on the train came from. Just as he was enjoying the orange setting sun glinting off of a large pond in the distance, everything went black.

This happened multiple times along their trip. The train would dart in and out of tunnels that had been carved through mountains to make train routes faster. During these times, everything in the car would go dark. The train had no lanterns because the darkness never lasted more than a few minutes. But those minutes were the slowest parts of the train ride. Shail could hear occasional coughs, sneezes, or snores over the train's screeching wheels and chugging axles. But he couldn't see what was happening, and it unnerved him.

The train ride took a couple of days. Some Dwarves stretched out on benches to sleep, others lay on the floor, probably out of fear of falling off of the bench in their sleep and waking up in pain. Shail lifted his bag up to use as a pillow. Occasionally he woke to find that it had slipped from his lap and he was using the stiff shoulder of his benchmate.

Eventually, the train rumbled to a halt. Shail looked out of the window to see a bright sun beaming down on a sea of wooden sheds in front of the mountainside. As Dwarves filed out, Shail heaved his bag off of the ground and threw it over his shoulder.

Outside, the sky was bright orange, yellow, and red. A Dwarf, with a neatly trimmed brown beard and slicked-back hair, bellowed orders. "Find the row with your number. Follow that row. You will find a shack with your name on the front. Newcomers will start work tomorrow at dawn."

Shail strolled down the line alone, having lost his teammate in the throng of other Dwarves. He relished being able to stretch his legs. He caught the first hints of rocky dust from the mines. Shail wanted to dance from how happy he was, being feet from the mountain, the mine, and the best job ever.

He found row 8. The rows were short, only housing half a dozen Dwarves for each time. Shail didn't see anybody else out in his row. He trudged down the row until he came upon an old wooden box with his name scratched into the front door. Shail pushed the door. The place seemed even smaller on the inside. There was barely enough room for a bedroll. A hook stuck out from the far wall, only a few feet away. Shail hung his bag up and began rummaging through it to organize his things.

After a couple of hours, the place was pretty well set up. An oil lantern hung from the hook at the end. A bedroll stretched out, along the wall, underneath it. His boots rested by the front door. Shail had used some twine to fashion a clothesline along the length of the space. This was it, home away from home.

CHAPTER 3

Going Down

Today was my first time being down in the mines.
I can't wait to go under again.

"Get a move on," shouted an older, gruff-looking Dwarf. He controlled the crank for the lift. Shail, along with two other Dwarves, crammed into the rusty metal cage with their rucksacks slung onto their backs. Shail looked to be the youngest, and cleanest, in the group.

The lift operator clunked the crank down until it covered the number 10. "Just two more floors to go, boys. Then we can get out of this pit." The other Dwarves around Shail grunted and groaned in response. His eyebrows stitched together as he glanced at each of them. No one showed the energy that he carried. He was full of youthful excitement, fresh out of a safe school in a society that valued the many riches from the depths of Mingun. Adrenaline filled Shail's veins as the lift operator punched a large button above the crank. The metal cage jolted awake. It began its laboured journey down into the depth of the Dwarf mine.

Shail watched the sunlight from the surface fade into a small dot high above his head. Darkness surrounded the four short, husky men. Sighs, grunts, and snuffles echoed off the tight rocky walls. The lift screeched down the shaft.

Bright torchlight cascaded into the cage as it crept past a previously used level of the mine. Finally, the lift jolted to a stop at one of these warm entrances.

"Get on your way now," instructed the operator. The Dwarf closest to the lift's doors pried their iron aside. The three passengers filed off. The lift operator slammed the doors shut again, cranked his lever back up to 1, and ascended back to the surface.

Shail watched the lift until it rose out of sight. When he turned around, the other passengers had disappeared. Torch-lit tunnels branched off in a multitude of directions. Shail's eyes scanned each identical tunnel. He realized he had no idea where to go or what to do. There was no map, no training, and no guide. All he learned in school was how to dig and extract.

A loud, low voice rumbled through the passages. From around a corner came a Dwarf, who looked to be around Shail's father's age. He had long straight black hair, speckled with strands of ashy grey.

"I 'spect more frum you this seasun, Boolg. So, you better not disappoint me or..." he stopped his ranting when he noticed Shail. "Wha' a' you doin' just standin' 'round 'ere?" His accent made it clear that he did not come from the same side of the mountain as Shail.

"Sorry, sorry. I just got down here and—" said Shail.

"Ooh a' you?" said the stranger as he swaggered toward Shail.

"P-pardon?" Shail fidgeted with the string that held his cotton shirt closed.

"You new 'ere?" The Dwarf squinted at Shail, mere inches from the young Dwarf's face.

"Yes, my name's Shail." He extended a hand to the other Dwarf.

"Mugsy." He gave Shail's hand a firm shake. "I'm the one supervisen' this floor. What's yur number?" Shail wiped black grime onto his pants.

"Um... Eight?"

"You ain't sure?" Mugsy shook his head and sighed. He pulled out a small notebook from the breast pocket of his leather vest. "Eight'd be this way." He pulled a torch off of the wall and lead Shail through the maze of tunnels. Sharp edges of grey, red, and brown rock jutted out from the angular walls.

Scratches from previous seasons of digging marred the surfaces of rock. Occasional holes showed where other Dwarves found minerals. The two Dwarves descended further and further into the mines. Indistinguishable voices reverberated up from the tunnel's depths. Mugsy and Shail rounded a curve in the tunnel.

A bright warm glow emanated from up ahead. Three figures stood at the end. "'Ere you are. Team eight. This is yur group fer the next few months. So get used to 'em." Mugsy nodded and tromped back the way he came. One of the Dwarves, with all grey hair and a face covered in wrinkles, glanced over his shoulder at Shail. The other Dwarves ignored the newcomer's presence. They examined a small opal gem peeking out of the rock.

"Hi, I'm Shail." He smiled, outstretching a hand to the old man. A wide grin exposed the Dwarf's missing teeth. He shuffled over, using his pickaxe as a cane, and greeted Shail with a weak shake from a veiny hand.

"Hello there young fellow. Shail, you say, what an interesting name. Call me Gadol. These other men here are Rukk and Mycka." Gadol's frail finger gestured to the nearest Dwarf, middle-aged and husky, with electric blond hair. Then Gadol pointed at a young Dwarf around Shail's age who had scruffy black hair. It was the same Dwarf Shail sat next to for the train ride over.

"So, you're the replacement, huh? So young and fresh. You sure you're old enough to be workin' down 'ere?" Rukk poked at Shail with the pointed end of his sharp pick.

"Please calm yourself," said Gadol, lowering Rukk's tool.

"What's wrong with me?" Shail looked at Gadol with some surprise. Rukk sneered and returned to prying out the gem.

Shail smiled at Mycka as his quiet benchmate turned around, grabbed a canister from his bag and took a swig. Mycka give a slight wave before getting back to work.

"You're a first-timer down here, just like Mycka?" Gadol patted Shail's shoulder.

"Yup, I'm very happy to be here."

"Well, just be careful, Shail, and remember your training. We don't want anybody getting hurt so far from the surface." Gadol gave him another big, toothless smile.

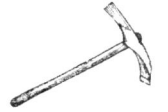

CHAPTER 4

Gas Leak

They evacuated the mines.

Over the next few weeks, Shail became better acquainted with his colleagues and settled into a normal work routine. When he went into work today everything felt normal. His team would expand their tunnel further into the mountain and excavate any gems and ore they found along the way. These would be placed in a cart and taken to the main lift. There it would be assessed and then sent up to the surface if it passed.

But, upon entering his tunnel, Shail noticed something peculiar. There was an odd noise. Shail was used to being the first one on site. He didn't like his brain being rattled awake by the loud, echoing clangs of pickaxes pounding at rock. He enjoyed coming down, lighting all the torches, and listening to the little Mornries sing their first-light songs.

Mornries are little, pudgy yellow birds. They prosper in flocks that dart around forests, gathering seeds, nuts, and berries. At dawn, their sweet songs can be heard for miles. Many villages cropped up around the mountains, cutting down the forests caught the Mornries. The Dwarves were the first to cage them and enjoy their melodies indoors. Many began bringing the caged song birds into the mines, to brighten their moods. And, they found that the little birds could detect gas leaks. As a symbol of sunlight and savior, the Dwarves mastered the technique of caging the little yellow birds and lining their tunnels with them.

Shail lit each wall-mounted-torch that he passed that morning. But he did not hear the Mornries. Instead, he heard the sound of something's claws scraping against rock. It darted down the tunnel, away from Shail.

"Hello?" he whispered into the darkness ahead. A skittering sound echoed off the hard, rocky walls. Shail tried to shrug it off. I'm sure bugs, bats or mole rats get into the mines occasionally, all lost, blind, and confused, he told himself. Shail lit the next few torches down to the end of the tunnel. Nothing was there. He set his torch into an empty metal ringlet on the left side of the tunnel and pulled his rucksack off of his back. Shail put on his steel helmet, heaved out his week-old pickaxe, and planted his feet for the first swing of the day.

He froze. The pickaxe scraped the wall, tilted sideways, and fell to the cold stony floor. Shail's hands turned white from gripping the pick's handle so hard. He slowly looked over his shoulder at the nearest bird cage. The tiny, grey, wire cage hung from a hook driven into the cave's wall. Inside, two tiny dishes contained alchemical everlasting food and water. A thin, wrought-iron perch bisected the middle of the cage. The door hung from one of its two hinges. The little golden bird was missing. Shail's green eyes grew large. He jogged up the tunnel to check the next cage. Missing too. He panicked and bolted past empty cage after empty cage. Finally, he found a bird. It lay still on its back, at the bottom of its cage.

"Gas leak. Gas leak. Everybody get out. There's a gas leak!" A man's voice resounded through the mine. Shail ran as hard and fast as he could. His heart pounded. Tears welled up from fear. Shail charged into the already cramped lift. A long, slow, clunky ride carried him to the surface. Eventually, all of the Dwarves were evacuated from the mines and sent home.

CHAPTER 5

The Cavern

We found the motherlode today.

By dawn the next morning, the mines were safe to return to. Shail got ready as soon as he heard. He was impressed with how quickly the company handled such an extreme problem. The Dwarf threw on one of his many identical sets of white cotton shirts and brown cotton pants. He braided his long red beard. Shail shoved each woolen-socked-foot into a steel-toed boot and headed to work.

The day before, in his panic, he forgot to grab his pickaxe and rucksack. So Shail prayed to the dwarven god, Bouldigon, that his tools would still be where he had left then.

Wearily Shail descended into the mines. He checked each caged bird. They sang sweet songs as Shail lit the torch across from their cages. When he reached the end of his tunnel, Shail found his pack lying on the ground. Everything inside of it was strewn about the floor.

Shail's canteen lay open on its side. Crumbs coated the area around his torn-up rations. He collected the bits of ration casings. Shail shoved the scraps and canteen back into his sack. He glanced around for his pickaxe. But it was nowhere in sight. Throwing his pack over his shoulder, he trudged back up the long tunnel to get a new pick. Along the way, Shail passed Rukk.

"Mornin'," Rukk grumbled.

"Hey Rukk." Shail greeted him with a nod. "I got everything set in the tunnel so you are good to start mining."

Rukk mumbled something back as he trudged down the shaft. Shail ignored him and marched on to the entry cavern. When he got there the lift arrived, its rusty doors being wrenched open by his new foreman. Mugsy left the mining company when the gas leak happened.

Shail forfeited five small copper disks to the still-groggy

foreman. He pulled out the most decent looking pick from the bunch. Shail nodded at his foreman and jogged off to his tunnel again.

As he neared the end of his tunnel, Shail did not hear anybody working. Instead, hushed voices drifted up. Rounding the last corner, he noticed his three teammates clustered around a spot on the right side of the tunnel.

"What are you all looking at?"

"Shh, we're listenin,'" Rukk said, motioning for Shail to come closer.

"Listening for what?" Shail whispered.

"I found a cave. I did," said Mycka, nodding.

"Very interesting indeed," said Gadol.

Shail peered into a hole the size of his head. Darkness enveloped the cavernous space. At the opposite side, a larger hole let in a glow. He squinted at the bright spot, its source of light flickered.

"I think that other hole leads into one of our mine's tunnels," Shail whispered. A black mass darted across the light. Shail jumped back, bumping into Gadol.

"Wooh!" Gadol stumbled back and outstretched his arms to regain his balance. Shaken, the old Dwarf stood and rested his weight on his pickaxe's metal end. "What was that for, sonny?"

"Sorry, I just..." Shail glanced back at the hole. "It looked like something ran past and blocked out the light." Gadol fidgeted, his eyes fixated on the hole. Rukk let out a bellowing laugh.

"You're so easy ta spook. T'was probably just a Dwarf in dee other tunnel." He chuckled a little more and slapped Shail on the back. "Let's get ta work." The strong Dwarf lifted his pick over his shoulder. The other Dwarves took a few steps back. Rukk swung the sharp tool and dug it deep into the rock just above the hole. He yanked it out. Chunks of rock crumbled, expanding their hole into the cavern. "We gotta check dee cave fer riches," Rukk said as he took another swing and tore more rock out of place.

Finally, the hole was made large enough for the Dwarves to fit through. Each of them grabbed a torch, or lit their lantern, before entering the dark cavern. They filed inside, one by one. The ceiling was fairly low but still allowed the Dwarves to stand erect; a Human would probably have to crouch. The group dispersed to inspect every crack and corner of the wide space.

Shail wedged himself into a crack that barely fit him when he turned sideways. He finished scanning the surfaces and was about to squeeze out when he saw a large black mass coming towards him. Panic flooded through him. He tried to shine light on the monstrosity but the arm with his torch was on the opposite side and he couldn't squeeze it around himself in such a tight space.

"Help, help. Guys you have to help me! There's something over here. It's coming right for me," Shail screamed. He shut his eyes, afraid to see the creature. Then, he heard laughter.

"Yer a dingus," exclaimed Rukk. Shail opened his eyes. Rukk sat on the ground, laughing, with a large black cloak covering him. Shail let out a long breath. Gadol shuffled forward and helped ease his shaken companion out of the tight crack. The old man brushed dust off of Shail's clothes.

"You screamed like a girl, you did," Mycka whooped. He pointed at Shail and laughed some more. Rukk picked himself up and slapped Shail on the back.

"Dat was good. Tanks fur da laugh," he said. The four

Dwarves returned to the cavern's main space. Rukk wandered over to a small, blue gem, stuck in the wall. Mycka and Gadol went to the far side, becoming a little glowing spot, leaving Shail alone.

Shail wandered off to a new section of the cavern. He followed a long winding passageway deep into the dark, cool, rocky depths of the mountain. Every so often his path branched off, turning into two or three separate tunnels; each time he took the path on the right. Along his way, Shail found small gems that he carefully evacuated from the wall, floor, or ceiling. As he wandered along, he could have sworn he heard something following him. But his torch's light did not show any creatures. Eventually, he ran into a dead end.

"Well, that was a fairly fruitful exploration," Shail mumbled to himself. He wandered back out of the tunnels. Shail loosened the drawstring of a small bag. "I must tell the others about these passages so that we can mine the gems out more quickly." The Dwarf had a warm sense of pleasure as he admired the rainbow-like multitude of pinhead-sized gems.

When Shail returned to the main space, two figures holding torches stood at the hole that they had made to get in. He could hear whispers coming from Mycka and Rukk.

"I found a network of tunnels over there that we should all check out," Shail offered, gesturing in the direction he came from. The two continued whispering, ignoring Shail's presence. "Hey." Still no response. "Helloooo? Am I invisible?" Shail grasped Mycka's shoulder and gave it a shake. Mycka spun around wide-eyed. "What happened? Where is Gadol? Did you find enough gems to send a cart up already?" Shail grew excited. A grin spread across his face at the latter. But the happiness faded as Mycka stared back blankly.

"I don't really know, ya know?" Mycka stammered. Rukk shook off his shock and slapped Mycka on the back of the head.

"Dun be eh wimp," he said with a scoff before exiting the cavern. Mycka turned to follow him out. But Shail stopped him.

"Hey, what is going on?" Shail's eyebrows stitched together.

"Gadol went into a tunnel branching off from this cavern, he did. He was gone for a while, he was. Yeah, a long while. Rukk and I were just mining away, we were. Suddenly, Gadol screamed. You didn't hear it?" Mycka paused. Shail shook his head. "You didn't? Well, Gadol did a lot more screaming before we saw him, oh yes he did. The old man ran through here faster than I've ever seen him move before. And he was yelling, he was. Wailing to Bouldigon about something he saw. But he got out of here so fast—" Mycka's eyes searched the darkness of the cavern around them. "We didn't have time to ask him what he saw. But, you know, he's old. He has been in the mines a long time. Maybe it was nothing; maybe he is just seeing things..." Mycka's hand, holding the torch, trembled. Shail put an arm around Mycka. The two of them went back into the main tunnel.

The three remaining Dwarves went back to mining away at their main tunnel. Mycka continued to eye the small, ominous entrance into the cavern. Eventually, Rukk got fed up with the distraction. He took a large rock and rolled it in front of the hole, blocking it up so that no creatures could enter or exit. Rukk became somewhat uneasy for the rest of the day after that. Nobody talked about what had happened. But curiosity nagged at the back of Shail's thoughts. Questions like, what had Gadol seen? Why was he so scared? Is he going to come back? whirred around in his head. But, even if he asked them, his team clearly wanted to ignore the issue.

Shail had never thought of the mines as a particularly scary sort of place. School prepared everybody for the possibility of cave-ins or gas leaks. But, the thought of dangerous creatures living so deep underground seemed like an impossible idea.

The Dwarves managed to excavate a decent amount of ore and gems that day, especially thanks to Shail's large find in the cavern. Shail's team felt drawn to excavate the rest of the riches hidden in the cavern. But, fear of the unknown drove the thoughts away. When their shift ended, each Dwarf packed up their belongings and raced out of the mines. And as each one passed the blocked hole in the wall, they eyed it uneasily.

CHAPTER 6

Old and Shaken

I have never seen a man so scared before...

Shail woke up and sluggishly went about his morning routine. By the time he got out the door he suspected his other team members had already beat him to the mines. The Dwarf slunk through the rows of tiny cabins. The lift screeched as it took him down. The glow from the torches seemed dimmer that day. Passing by, he glanced at the cavern's entrance. Shail gave a sigh of relief. The large rock still rested in front of the hole. When he got to the end of the tunnel, only Rukk was there.

"Hi Rukk, where is everybody else?" Shail glanced around for traces of the other's. But no belongings lay about besides Rukk's.

"Wimps, all of 'em," the Dwarf grumbled back as he continued breaking away chunks of rock. "Sorry?" Shail's brow creased and a frown wavered on his lips. He set his pack down against a side of the tunnel. He sifted through it for his helmet, pick, and lantern. Then he pulled out his canteen and took a swig before offering it to Rukk. The older Dwarf took no notice of the offering, staying fixated on the wall in front of him.

"Didn't 'spect ya ta show up. Doubt dem uda two be comin'. Lookin' like da young be just as weak as da old." Rukk's actions grew rough. His pick dug deeper into the wall and at a more irate pace.

"Calm down, Rukk," Shail said, and rested a hand on his shoulder. Rukk spun around. His face was bright red. Throbbing veins stuck out.

"No, dis's ridic'lous!" Rukk's voice boomed through the tunnel. Shail took a step back, his eyes wide. "Dem bois betta be 'ere 'fore dis day is t'rough or I'll..." His echoes faded down the tunnel. Rukk's eyes fixated on something over Shail's shoulder.

"What is it, Rukk?" Slowly, Shail turned around. A figure

stood in the shadows. Shail froze. His palms grew sweaty. Silence passed for a few moments as the two Dwarves and the stranger stared back at one another. Then, the figure took a slow, heavy step. Then another. And another. Shail's heart raced in his chest. Is this what Gadol was scared of? Will it kill us? It's blocking our exit. What do I do? Throw my pick at it? But then it can use my pick to kill me. Hope Rukk has something that can kill it? Throw fire at it? The possibilities and uncertainties raced through Shail's head as the dark figure slowly moved closer. Then, it entered a torch's light.

"Gadol…" came Rukk's hushed voice. The two Dwarves stared at their companion.
"I didn't think you would come back after yesterday…" Shail sighed as relief overcame the adrenaline in his system. Gadol silently approached. He rested his pack next to Shail's. He pulled out his pickaxe and moved next to Rukk to begin mining. Rukk still stood facing Shail, his mouth hanging open.

After a few moments, Rukk and Shail shook off their disbelief. They wearily joined Gadol in extending their tunnel. Every so often the two younger Dwarves gave each other questioning looks while nudging their head at Gadol. The older Dwarf's eyes seemed glazed over and his mind did not seem with them. Hours passed with this uneasy mining. Occasionally gems were found. But they were small and fragile, making them easy to crack or chip, and therefore useless.

"Damn dis pick," Rukk exclaimed, throwing his tool to the ground. It hit the floor of the tunnel and tumbled onto its side. "Useless t'ing can't get dese gems out w'itout breakin' 'em," he groaned and slumped to the floor, intertwining his fingers behind his head.

"It's not just you, Rukk." Shail took a break, dismayed by his own misfortunes and now his colleague's frustration.

"I can't work wit' dis husk next ta me." He gave Gadol a dirty look. "Damned old timer shouldn't be down 'ere. Shoulda just let dem shadows scare ya out!" Rukk stood up, puffing up his muscles as he snarled out each word at the old man. Then he spat at Gadol's feet, spun around, and tromped up the tunnel.

"Gadol, I'm sorry. I..." said Shail. The old man gently set down his pickaxe and used it as a cane to hobble over to Shail. Slowly, he lowered himself onto a rock next to the young Dwarf.

"It is quite alright. Rukk is just scared."

"Scared?" Shail gazed at Gadol in bewilderment.

"We all express fear in very different ways. Rukk views it as a weakness and becomes frustrated at those who show weak emotions."

"Hmm." Shail looked down the tunnel where Rukk had gone. Gadol continued.

"What I saw yesterday was surely something to be afraid of. Have you ever heard of the Mezmurs?" His eyes still seemed glazed over as he stared at the wall opposite them. Shail shook his head. "Ah, well, I suppose I am showing my age. This tale is quite old now I suppose. Every child knew it when I was growing up. Parents told it to their children so that they would not go exploring in the mines after dark. Too many accidents would happen, you see..." said the old man with a crackly voice.

"Back when I was but a child, my mother would tuck me into bed at night and tell me stories. Some were lovely fables about powerful wizards who saved their castle from an evil sorcerer; others told of a time when a vast orc army tried to take over the lands. But beneath all of these wondrous stories lay important lessons that my mother would try to instill in me at a young age. One of these tales stuck with me to this day. It was told by every dwarvish mother to their child. She called them Mezmurs."

CHAPTER 7

Wives' Tale

My mother told me a story like this once.
It kept me up all night.

"These creatures stand as tall as an adult Dwarf's waist. And they run around on two legs, unlike other animals. Their skin is as tough as leather and extremely pale, almost translucent. It sags across the creature's body, making the bones of its slender figure stand out even more. The fingers on them are grotesque; long and spindly like a daddy-long-legs. Three small nubs along each finger are the joints where they can bend. These allow it to grasp and cause more gruesome attacks with its long claws. Their somewhat short feet create an odd contrast with the long fingers. But, sharp claws extend from each stumpy toe; they scratch the ground as they scurry around underground. Though, the worst part about them is their face. A long snout gives them a strong sense of smell in the dark. Short, pointed ears perch on either side of their head but they do little to aid the creature. Saucer-sized orbs, which shimmer like cat eyes in the dark, catch every tiny movement in the caverns where they reside.

"My mother never spoke of where they came from or how they lived in mines for so long. But, she made it clear that their favorite food was young Dwarves. The moral of the story was to keep children away from the mines. And boy, did this story work on a lot of us."

One night, a young boy decided to sneak out of his family's home and go exploring. He would sneak out every so often and usually get caught by his mother the next morning when she discovered mud on his pant legs or scratches from thorns on his hands. But, the boy did not care about the punishments his mother gave him or the warnings she would preach about bad men or monsters. On this particular night it was chilly and raining, not hard mind you, just a slight drizzle. The boy slipped on his rubber boots and a thick poncho his mother had knitted him for his birthday a week earlier. Out he went, into the night, on his own to go exploring.

His small form made it easy for him to dart through the shadows of his village. Once he crossed the picket-fenced threshold, the boy relaxed. Nobody from the village had ever spotted him at this distance before. He sloshed through the mud on the side of the road and gazed around at the quiet, dark landscape around him. Tall, bushy trees took on the figures of ogres. Large rocks stuck in the ground were the boulders they lobbed at him. Luckily they always missed, night after night. Leafless thorny bushes were old, hunched over men, who had grand stories to tell about their adventures, of fighting off dragons and gryphons, when they were young.

The boy wandered over to the old village graveyard. He weaved through the cracked, weathered tombstones. The cold crept under his thick layers of clothing. Goosebumps prickled his arms and legs. The further into the graveyard he went, the more of an eerie feeling crept over the boy. He felt eyes watching the back of his head. But every time he turned around, nothing was there.

"My mother always said it was the eyes of his ancestors watching him, scolding him for being out, and trying to make him go home before something bad happened."

The boy visited the graveyard many times and never ran into danger before. And so he grew more adventurous. His father had always warned him to stay away from the mines until he was of age to work in them, and, while traipsing through the graveyard that night, those ramblings emerged from the back of his mind. Intrigued by the idea of the mines, the boy headed west.

"This will be great," the boy said, only loud enough for

his own ears to hear. "I know father and mother worry about me and all, but it's only a few more years until I'm old enough to start working. Father always says that the more one knows about the world, the longer they'll survive. So, playing in the mines before I start working makes sense because I'll be safer once I have to spend all day every day underground." The boy began to feel more confident.

He rubbed out the damp cold that seeped into his layers. Looking up at the moon, the boy checked the time. Only a couple hours had elapsed since he'd left home. He still had plenty of time before his mother would rise and begin getting ready for work. He knew very well that she would know he had been out all night. But he would be home and safe, so her nagging would cease before noon.

When the boy reached the mines, he tiptoed and slunk around the rocks and shrubs from fifty feet away. A light fog set in making his clothes damp and heavy. Gusts of wind whirled by. They howled in the tunnels that weaved through the mountainside. The boy, startled by booming sounds, shook. He blamed it on the chilly air. Slowly, he crept closer and closer to the cavern's entrance.

Keeping his eyes peeled with each inch he moved closer, the boy eventually got to the giant hole in the rock. He was surprised by how little machinery lay about. The boy expected to find large burrowing machines or piles of glistening pickaxes. He would have hours of fun. But no such luck. Instead, heaps of rubble towered around the entryway. With all the dirt that had been removed, it seemed like the tunnels would go on forever.

The boy peeked around the edge of the gaping rocky maw. It was dark inside. A shiver wriggled down his spine.

Another booming gusty roar bellowed out from inside the mines. The boy stood at the entrance, eyes pinched shut, hands over cold ears, shaking. But his curiosity eventually overcame his nerves.

Creeping into the darkness of the main cavern, feeling his way along the cold, stony walls, the boy could see a dim light far down one of the tunnels. A sense of warmth and comfort seemed to emanate from the distant speck so the boy made his way to it. Nearing the light, the boy realized it was the flickering firelight of a lantern. Reaching up, and taking the lantern off of its hook. Dark, damp rock encircled the boy. Droplets of water hung from points above him and fell and formed occasional puddles underfoot. Luckily, the boy was wearing his rain boots so he did not have to worry about water soaking into his socks.

He shifted to shine the light further down the tunnel he was in and saw nothing but rock and darkness. But now that he had a light, the boy had more of a reason to stay in the tunnels and explore that night. He meandered deeper into the mines.

Uneven, sharp, deep-coloured rock surrounded him. Scratchings marred the walls where worker's pickaxes scratched the rock during the day. While admiring one of these etchings, the boy slipped in one of the slick puddles on the tunnel's floor. He winced as he landed hard on his back, clutching the lantern rather than brace his fall. The boy couldn't afford to break his light source, for he feared that without it he would be lost in the tunnels forever.

Slowly, he picked himself up and brushed himself off. Water soaked the butt of his pants, but that was fine, considering his lantern was still unbroken. Looking up, the boy noticed something small and fluffy dart around the corner ahead. Some sort of rat.

"Hey…" he whispered, crouching down. "Hey… come here. Don't worry, I won't hurt you," the boy coaxed. He cooed for a while, trying to coax out whatever was hiding. The boy had almost given up and began to stand, when a small puffy head peaked out from around the corner.

Small, beady eyes peaked out of thick, soft-looking fur, like snow. Four little feet, grey from the grime in the tunnels, poked out from its fluff-ball body. It could fit in the palm of a Dwarf's hand. The boy inched closer to the creature.

"Are you lost?" It tilted its head to the side in response. The boy outstretched a hand, palm up.

"Peep!" chirped the creature. It scurried around the corner.

"Hey, wait. Let me help you get out of here," the boy hollered down the tunnel where the creature had gone. Standing up, he brushed himself off, took hold of his lantern again and jogged after the creature. He could hear peeps and chirps echoing inside the tunnel ahead of him. He tried to follow the creature. Occasionally, he caught a glimpse of some white fur on the border of his ring of light.

The boy followed the creature further and further into the tunnels, paying little attention to where he was going.

Suddenly, the boy slipped. He landed on his stomach, catching himself with his hands. But the floor underneath was cold and slick. The boy slid down. The boy neglected to see the slimy ground beneath him or the oncoming dip in the tunnel.

The boy screamed a mixture of surprise and disgust. He lifted his hands to shield his face, worried about slamming into a rock wall. His screaming echoed through the tunnels, mixed with the squelching sounds of the muck underneath him.

Finally, the boy felt his body level out and the slippery feeling underneath him had gone away. But now it was replaced by dry bumpy rock. The boy's body twisted and turned as it was thrown around by dips and peaks in the ground. He heard the smashing of something fragile just before skidding to a stop.

The boy blinked before realizing that his eyes were open. He could see, but everything was black. He grasped around for his lantern, desperate to find his way out now. Then it occurred to him that the smash he had heard when he was sliding was his lantern breaking. The boy squeezed his eyes shut as he prayed to any god that might be listening for help. For a few moments he curled into a ball and rocked himself back and forth. He thought of his mother and how much he wished he had listened to her warnings, and his father, who had made it clear that the mines were meant for adults.

His body ached from the long, hard fall and spots of his skin seared where sharp rocks had nipped at his soft flesh. "How will I get home when I am so sore? And without a light?! I can't even go back the way I came because that slope is way too slippery." His mind raced, trying to come up with some idea of how to get home, his ears picked up a familiar sound. It was the squeaks and chirps of the fluffy, white creature that had gotten him into this awful situation.

"Hello?" The boy's voice echoed off cold, lonely tunnel walls, deep into the mountain's mines. Slowly, he managed to get himself upright and standing. "Hello?" he asked again.

A few chirps and clicks came from ahead of him, or so they sounded. The boy stretched his arms out in front of him and meandered through the dark tunnel after the creature again. Seeing as it was just the boy and the creature, he tried to have a conversation. Talking made him feeling calmer.

"Are you from here? Do you know the way out? I really need to get home. My mother will be worrying soon." The occasional remark seemed to evoke a vocal response from the creature, allowing the boy to follow it more easily.

The two traversed their way through the mines for a long time. The boy was terrified with every passing second. Then, a noise from up ahead, a sort of grunting mingled with the clangs of rock being hit by something metal. The boy jumped from the faint, distant echoes. He filled with excitement at the thought that somebody else was down here. He would go home after all and everything would be fine.

"Come on little guy, let's get out of here," the boy said happily to the creature. It chirped but this time the sound came from behind the boy. "Oh, don't be scared. It's just a miner, and with his help we can both go home to our families."

The boy wandered through the darkness, following the sounds of mining while the creature stayed close at his ankles. Feeling his way around a corner, the boy saw a small glow flickering up ahead. He gasped.

"A torch," he mumbled. Then the boy began jogging. His body complained from the fall but the boy ignored it as best he could. "Hello? Sir? Help!" he yelled down the tunnel. The mining stopped and the boy could hear multiple voices grunting and mumbling.

"I'm sorry but I need help. I got lost in these mines a few hours ago and need to go home. Can you show me the way out please? I brought a lantern but it broke a while ago so I can't find my way out of all these dark and twisty tunnels." The boy limped closer and closer to the light. He could see a few large figures huddled together in the shadows on the opposite side of the torch. The boy stopped at the edge of the firelight. "Um… hello?" The grunting stopped. "Excuse me? Please help me."

The closest figure waddled around to face the boy and took a few laboured steps toward him. Two plods of bare feet on rock sounded, followed by the knock of something wooden. When the creature stepped into the light of the torch, only a couple feet away from the boy, a scream echoed through the caverns. The creature that stood before the boy was a grotesque, old Mezmur. The wooden, knocking sound came from a rusty, bloody pickaxe that it used for a cane. Letting out another scream, the boy spun around on his heels and ran into another Mezmur.

He screamed even more, shoving at the monster, but it didn't budge, or twitch, or even blink from the boy's commotion. It just stared back at him with its bulbous cat-like eyes. For a second, the boy caught a glimpse of the creature in front of him as the white fluffy thing that he had been following. What the boy didn't know was that this white fluffy creature lived in the mines. It used psionics, mind manipulating magic, to lure the boy into a false sense of security. The boy opened his mouth to let out another scream. But he felt compelled to close his mouth. He did so, tense from fear. The monstrosity in front of him gave a large, pointy-toothed grin. Then, it chomped onto the boy's arm.

Some Dwarves say that they heard the faint screams of a child echoing up from deep in the mines when they went to work that morning. A couple of days later, search parties scoured the mines to find the missing boy. But all they ever found was a broken lantern and one of the boy's small, rubber boots in front of a freshly caved-in tunnel.

CHAPTER 8

Did You See Them?

Rukk refuses to believe.
But I'm not so sure.

"That cavern that we found... I think it's the same one from the story. Over my years of mining, I have heard others tell tales vastly different than mine. But they all talk about a bipedal rat-like creature that lives in colonies deep in the mountains." Gadol massaged his hands together. Then rubbed the sweat from them onto his pants. Shail sighed.

"They're just fables though, you said so yourself. These are all just stories made to keep kids out of the mines..."

"No... no! They are real, boy. Trust me. I saw one." Gadol grasped Shail's shoulders and shook him.

"Saw one? You mean a Mezmur?" The colour drained from Shail's face.

"I told the foreman what I saw yesterday. He stopped me on my way out and wouldn't let me pass until I told him what had shaken me so." At that moment, Rukk showed up.

"Gadol was just telling me how he thinks there are Mezmurs in these mines," said Shail.

"Mezmurs?" Rukk burst into laughter. Shail looked at Gadol. He had a very dejected expression. "Dem mongrels been 'stinct fer years." He chuckled some more as he flung open the top of his bag and pulled out his pickaxe.

"Extinct?" Shail cocked a brow. "Gadol was telling me a children's fable about them. He is convinced he has seen one and that they are real."

"A fable?" Rukk boomed. He spun around, took three swift strides, and shoved a fat finger in Shail's face. "I be damned if dem crittas came out of some 'ere story."

"So I'm not crazy... You've seen them too!" Gadol quavered onto his feet. He grinned a mad, wide smile that showed gaps in his teeth.

"Pfft, I never saw 'em. Dey been gone fer so long dat nobody seen 'em in ages."

"Oh, I did," the old Dwarf said. "It was small, small as a lop ear's tail and it looked fluffy as a dandelion field in full bloom. Mind you, it was dark in those caves but I know what I saw."

"Well, if you did truly see what ya say ya saw then it be best ta warn the foreman and get these 'ere mines closed down."

The old man nodded fervently at Rukk. He glanced at Shail before spinning around and hobbling up the tunnel as fast as he could.

"Is that true? Do the mines really need to be closed?" Shail's brow furrowed. Rukk laughed.

"Of course not boy! Dere be nuthin ta worry 'bout down 'ere but dat old man and da crazy t'ings 'ee t'inks 'ee sees." Shail warily picked up his axe and followed Rukk in mining their tunnel out further. Eventually, Mycka showed up for work as well, but nobody said a word to each other.

As the day eased by, the Dwarves worked in silence. The irregular clangs from their picks echoed through the cold tunnel. Around noon the mine's foreman came down to their tunnel. It was an odd sight.

"You're all doing a great job," said the foreman as he sifted through their findings. Shail turned around and gave the man a polite smile before taking a swig from his canteen and continuing to mine. "You boys know anything about some critter that's causing a stir in the mines? Got a guy who says the caverns you found are full of something nasty."

"Old coot's tellin' ya lies," Rukk turned around, set his pack down, and crossed his arms over the end of the handle. Shail and Mycka tried to ignore the conversation. "But, I told 'im that them Mezmurs been 'stinct fer years." He nodded. The foreman looked somewhat confused. He had trouble understanding Rukk through his thick accent.

"Riiight… okay, well how about one of you show me these caverns?" Shail and Mycka glanced at each other nervously.

"This 'eer's Shail. He'll take ya to 'em," Rukk placed a firm hand on Shail's shoulder. Shail looked at Rukk, bewildered. His complexion dropped a few shades as he stopped mining and slowly glanced over his shoulder at the foreman.

"Come on boy, I don't have all day," the foreman tapped his boot on the floor. Shail brought his pickaxe as he slunk past the foreman, back up the tunnel. The large rock still stood in the way of the hole they'd dug into the caverns. Shail had thought the blockage was sufficient before. But now, as he took a closer look, there were spaces that a small creature could easily scurry through. It took both Dwarves to shift the boulder to the side so that the foreman could fit. As they did so, Shail grew curious.

"Have you ever heard of these creatures called Mezmurs before?" The foreman chuckled.

"I'm surprised you haven't, boy. Not to worry though, just old wives' tales. There's no way anything can live trapped underground for so long." Once they got the boulder moved, the foreman took a step inside and turned on his lantern. "You coming, boy?"

"I'd rather wait out here, Sir," Shail hollered from around the boulder. He positioned himself so that when the time came or if anything happened, he could shove the boulder back into place. Shail stared at the wall opposite him, avoiding any contact with the cavern. He listened carefully. He was sure he heard the fore-

man call him a pansy amongst the thumping of his
steel-plated boots. The footsteps faded away. Shail recalled his fear
when he had been stuck in that crack in the cavern. The darkness
felt suffocating. He had never experienced claustrophobia before.
Shail gained some respect for the foreman. He had the courage to
check the cavern, all alone, and after hearing about magical,
rat-like creatures infesting the cavern.

CHAPTER 9

Another Closure

They trapped us down here!

Shail sat outside the cavern for a long time. Every so often, he could hear the foreman's boots plodding around the main area of the cavern, or the squeaks of his lantern swinging. At one point he could have sworn he heard the foreman talking.

"Are you alright in there, sir?" Shail yelled. No response. Then, the sound of glass shattering rang out from the cavern. Shail jumped up. "Sir? Excuse me? Are you okay?" He inched around the boulder and peeked into the darkness. He couldn't hear or see anything. Shail bolted down the mine shaft to Rukk and Mycka. He tried to explain through gasps of air, "foreman — danger — crashing — sound — hurt — Mezmurs!"

"Wha- wha- what are you saying?" Mycka shook. Rukk set his pick down and strode up the tunnel.

"Ugh, why didn't ya go in dere an' 'elp 'im? I gotta do everyt'ing ma self," he said. Shail trotted along behind. When they got to the cave entrance, Rukk paused.

"We shouldn't go in there..." Shail said. He leaned over to see a brief look of fear on Rukk's face. The older Dwarf shook off his concerns and took a step into the cavern.

"Be careful, Rukk." No sooner had these words left Shail's mouth when something made Rukk yelp and jump to the side. "What is it? What's wrong?" Shail began to panic. Rukk let out a sigh.

"It's the foreman." Both men emerged from the cavern.

"Well? What do you think? Is it Mezmurs?" Shail's eyes darted from the foreman to Rukk.

"Nothing's wrong with those caverns," the foreman said bluntly. "Another crew on the opposite side also opened a hole into this cavern. I'm sure it was just one of them that your co-worker saw. Don't worry about this cavern. It's not dangerous and you should finish excavating everything from it. Now get back to work." The foreman wandered off. A broken lantern swung from his hip.

"See? Told ya, boy," Rukk said to Shail. "Now, let's get Mycka and get da rest of dese gems out." Shail followed Rukk. But he kept glancing back. Something about that foreman had changed, but he couldn't figure out what. When they returned, Mycka had thrown all his belongings in his pack and was pacing in circles.

"So? What happened? Did the foreman say they're closing the mines? Did he?!" The young Dwarf was frantic.

"No, we gotta get da rest of dem gems in da cavern," Rukk stated as he collected his things.

"W-w-w-what?" Mycka looked like he might faint or cry or both. Shail didn't respond. He was as scared as Mycka. But if he let the young Dwarf see then he'd run off and never enter a mine again.

"Come on, boy," Rukk grabbed the handle of Mycka's bag and practically dragged the young Dwarf up the tunnel.

As they neared the cavern's entrance, Gadol came hurtling towards them, wielding a pickaxe. The weight of his rucksack almost toppled him over with each stride. "Come. You have to hurry," he shouted, waving his arms in the air.

"What's wrong?" Shail looked at the old Dwarf, concerned.

"We have to leave. They're closing the mines!"

"What?" they all exclaimed. Mycka bolted up the tunnel past all of them. Shail and Rukk exchanged a look before running off as well, leaving Gadol behind to limp back up the long, lonely tunnel.

When Shail reached the elevator, Mycka was, "let us up. This isn't fair!". Rukk was trying to pull him away from the lift's bars, "calm down Mycka. Yur actin' like a child.

"What's happening? Why won't the elevator doors open?" Shail tried to pry the metal doors apart with Mycka.

"Ugh, not you too..." said Rukk, letting go of Mycka. "Dey turned dis damn machine off wit'out getting' us out first."

"What are you talking about? It must just be jammed." Shail shook the bars in frustration and let out a tense groan. He paced in circles with his hands raised, fingers interlocked on top of his head.

"H-h-hey, get back here and help me. You have tɔ," Mycka said, trying to pry the doors open.

"Dey ain't gonna open, boy," Rukk said, moving forward and placing a hand on Mycka's shoulder.

"B-but why did they do this to us?" Mycka burst into tears as he hid his face in his hands.

"Because," a crackly voice from behind them said. The Dwarves spun around. It was the mine's foreman. "We're being hunted."

CHAPTER 10

The Hunt

Gadol is ranting off assumptions about the Mezmurs.
And the foreman seems to know more
than he is letting on.

"Hunted?" Shail stopped pacing and stared at the foreman, terrified.

"W-w-what are you talking about?" Mycka said from a red, puffy, tear-smeared face.

"He means that any one of us could have seen those creatures. They will not let us remember." Gadol finally caught up to the group.

"Ya closed dese mines 'cause of sum old story?" Rukk's eyebrows stitched together and a frown creased his face.

"I'm not sure it's that simple," the foreman sighed.

"Why da hell not?" Rukk's voice boomed as he took a few steps toward the foreman, fists clenched at his sides.

"Rukk, calm down," said Shail.

"I will not! Dis id'yot 'as trapped us all down 'ere all 'cause of an old man," he growled at Gadol.

"I did what was right," Gadol said. Rukk took a step toward the old Dwarf.

"It's true, calm down, boy," the foreman said, outstretching an arm to Rukk in a "stop" gesture. "What I saw…"

"You saw something? What? What did you see?" Mycka asked.

"Remember how I said that another team must have broken into the cavern on the other side?" Shail and Mycka nodded while Rukk stared at the foreman, frustrated. "Well, when I went to check on them, I couldn't find any of the crew. All of their packs were still there, but they'd disappeared."

"Well," Shail interjected, "hadn't you already given the order to evacuate?"

"No." The foreman shook his head. "After they had

disappeared was when I gave that order." Rukk noticed that Gadol had moved to Mycka's side and was comforting the young, fretful Dwarf.

"Hey, git 'way from 'im," he hollered as he strode over to the two and shoved Gadol away. The older Dwarf stumbled back, nearly falling over. Shail saw this and ran to the man's side, helping to steady him.

"What is wrong with you, Rukk?" Shail frowned.

"'Ee's de only one who says ee seen dem creatures." Rukk thrust a finger at Gadol.

"Is this true?" the foreman asked. Gadol nodded.

"Hang on. Did you not say, just a moment ago, that you saw something too?" Shail looked inquisitively at the foreman.

"I did start to say something like that. But I didn't see any creatures. Just thought I caught a glimpse of something moving in that cavern." The four Dwarves eyed their foreman warily.

"W-w-what if they're controlling Gadol? What then?" Mycka said, shaking. The Dwarves looked from one to the other.

"What did your mother tell you?" Shail said. Gadol shook his head.

"Nothing more than what I told you. I've never heard a story tell what happened to the victims." Shail turned his attention to the others.

"Rukk? Foreman? One of you must have some idea?" Rukk shook his head and rubbed Mycka's back.

"Beryl," mumbled the foreman.

"What?" Shail asked.

"My name's Beryl. Figure since you might be the last Dwarves I ever see, you should know my name."

"Okay, Beryl, know anything about why these creatures

are hunting us, or what will happen?"

"Stories all say something a little different. But the gist of it is that if they catch a hint of your smell in their territory then they hunt down your scent. It's easy for them to hunt you. They've adapted to hunting in the dark. Then, they eat you, slowly, and alive. These creatures often have trouble getting food because of how far underground they live. So they save as much of you as they can for as long as they can."

"They can control us though? What does that mean?" Shail asked.

"Of course, boy. All creatures do. These ones are said to have terrible hearing so they have adapted a sort of hive mind to communicate. As the ages have gone by they have evolved a very strong mind; one that is capable of psionics."

"Psionics?" Rukk stuttered.

"Yes, boy. The ability to control one's mind or alter another's thoughts and perceptions."

"How does that help them to hunt?" Shail stepped away from Gadol now.

"It's like in the story I told you," Gadol piped up. "They manipulate the mind of their prey to see them as something harmless, luring you into a false sense of..." He trailed off.

"What's wrong, old man?" Rukk sighed. He tromped over to Gadol and gave him a shake.

"Why?" Gadol mumbled.

"W-w-what did he say?" Mycka took a small step closer.

"What's wrong with him?" Beryl crossed his arms. Then, Gadol locked eyes with him. His old eyes were as wide as an owl's and full of some great terror that shook Gadol to his very core. "Is he always like this?"

"Why me?" Gadol asked.

"Speak up, ya old coot," said Rukk through clenched teeth.

"Why am I the only one who remembers seeing them?" Shail frowned.

"Well what exactly do you remember?"

"Nothing. I was in that cavern and I can just picture them clearly. It was only one. But it looked just like how my mother described them. They are so lanky, so menacing, so, so… hungry." Gadol looked pail.

"S-s-so we're just trapped down here with those things, until they come and take us to their den to slowly eat us? Huh?" Mycka's eyes darted around, scanning the tunnel entrances.

"Well, I suppose they won't let us up…" Shail said. "Hang on. The reason you kept us down here, Beryl, was because you thought we were being hunted. But, what's stopping everybody else from being hunted too? Why is it only us who are trapped down here?"

"Because they didn't break into their burrow!" Beryl said. Gadol sat down on the cold, hard ground and began moaning. This caused Mycka to burst into tears again.

"They can't just live off of Dwarves that accidently mine into their burrow though…" Shail added.

Gadol said, "The Mezmurs are rat-like creatures. It is likely that they eat moles, bats, and, of course, our Mornries, normally."

"But I also didn't see any Mezmurs when I was down there." Shail looked around cautiously, fixating on the tunnel that he had been working on.

"It's not a matter of whether you saw one," Beryl said.

"It's that one saw or smelled you. They have a hive mind, remember? Once one knows, then all of them learn a split second later. And even without that connection, they would have smelled that you had been in there when they all returned to their den that night."

"Dis is ridic'lous," Rukk said, shoving past Beryl and marching toward their tunnel.

"W-w-what're you doing?" Mycka said.

"Goin' ta prove dat dis is a lie."

"Wait, you can't just go running off down there." Shail ran over and grabbed Rukk's arm. Rukk yanked away and spun around.

"Like 'ell I can't! We're trapped down 'ere all 'cause of sum old wives' tale an' I'm not gonna put up wit' dis any longa," Rukk yelled at Shail, who gazed pleadingly back at him.

Beryl stepped forward. "Even if this is just some crazy story come true… You shouldn't go alone."

"Oh, so ya suggest we drag dee old man an' cry baby down ta get 'em ta shut up?" The three glanced back at their shaken companions that were curled up near the elevator shaft. Shail frowned and turned back to Rukk.

"Leave them here, but Beryl and I are going with you."

"Do wat ya want," Rukk sneered, spun around, and continued down the tunnel. Beryl followed closely behind. Shail jogged over to Mycka and Gadol, leaned down, and placed a hand on the younger's shoulder.

"We will be right back, you two. Just stay here and stay safe, because when we get back, all of us are getting out of here." Neither Dwarf looked at Shail or acknowledged his words, so he simply nodded and ran off down the tunnel, after them.

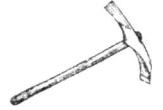

CHAPTER 11

Into The Dark

Team 9 must have been taken when the last "gas leak" happened.

Shail caught up to his companions just as they got to the entrance of the cavern. Beryl and Rukk peered into the darkness, quietly contemplating. "Is everything okay?" Shail asked as he pulled a torch off of the wall nearby.

"Shh… Do you hear that?" Beryl whispered into the darkness. Shail stepped closer and cocked his head to listen into the cavern.

"No… What am I supposed to be hearing?"

"See, yer just goin' crazy," Rukk said.

Beryl glanced at Rukk and then Shail before shrugging. "Guess it was nothing."

"Should we get our pickaxes in case—" Shail began.

"Come on, ya really t'ink der's sumthin' in dere?" said Rukk in frustration.

"If you want to," said Beryl, ignoring Rukk's complaint.

Shail ran further down the tunnel, his companions' bickering slowly disappearing behind him. When he rounded the dimly lit corner, he skidded to a stop. Everything that had been neatly packed into their bags, which had all been lying in a heap, was now strewn about the floor of the tunnel. Shail gasped and dashed over to his bag. He rummaged through it to see what remained.

His journal, a rag, some brushes and smaller excavating tools… Shail found that many of his rations were torn open. Only crumbs remained. Luckily, two survived the onslaught. He also found that his canteen had been left unopened, so that was another good sign. Shail realized that this was just like when the last gas leak happened.

Maybe that was when team 9 was killed. He was reminded of the disturbed man from the train ride to the mine.

That man was assigned team 9. His ramblings had warned Shail about a monster in the mines. That man knew what was going on, he survived an attack, and now it looks like they finally got him...

He collected what was left and trudged a few paces back up the tunnel, where a pickaxe lay on its side a few feet from their stuff. Shail bent down and hefted his tool over his shoulder, then tromped back up the tunnel to Rukk and Beryl.

"We should probably all go in together..." Shail rounded the corner and realized that neither Dwarf was waiting for him outside the cavern's entrance. "H-hello? Rukk? Beryl?" He poked his head into the darkness and called out. No reply other than his own voice returned.

"Maybe they went back to Gadol and Mycka," Shail thought aloud. He took a couple steps up the tunnel before pausing and glancing into the darkness. "But what if they went in there already? They don't know that those creatures might be wielding pickaxes." Shail gripped the handles of his pickaxe and torch tighter. "If I go in there, and they didn't, then the Mezmurs will get me for sure..." Shail took a few more steps up the tunnel. "I'll just check on Gadol and Mycka first..." He sprinted away from the tunnel and all the way up to the main cavern. Once safely in the bright torch light, Shail bent over and took a few moments to catch his breath. When he looked up, only Mycka was there. He was still huddled in a ball by the elevator shaft, shaking.

"Mycka?" Shail briskly moved to the younger Dwarf's side and knelt down.

"O-o-oh! Thank goodness you're back, thank you, thank you." He gave Shail a large, tight hug.

"I told you I'd come back..." Shail glanced around the

cavern. "But where's Gadol?" Mycka froze, the shaking ceased, and his eyes began frantically scanning the cavern. "W-w-where's Rukk… and Beryl, huh? Where are they?" Shail glanced around again.

"I'm not sure… I thought they might have come back here…" Mycka shook his head.

"Where did Gadol go?" Shail repeated. Mycka hid his face in his hands and moaned. "M-Mycka? What is it?" Shail dropped his torch and pickaxe so he could shake his companion by the shoulders.

"H-h-h-he's gooone," Mycka said through hiccupping sobs. Shail's eyes went wide and his fingers dug into Mycka's shoulders. The younger Dwarf winced. "Th-th-they to-ok him," he whined.

CHAPTER 12

One of Them

Gadol, Rukk, and Beryl have disappeared.
Without them,
we have no hope of getting out of here.

A shiver went down Shail's spine. "What? You mean they? Like the... the creatures?" Mycka nodded a little. "When? What did they look like? Are they the same as the legends? Where did they take him?" Shail stared at the entrances to each tunnel that branched off from their cavern, scanning for any signs of movement or sound.

Shail began to perspire as he stood in front of Mycka. Slowly, droplets formed and weaved their way down the contours of his face until they reached his chin and dripped off onto the cave's floor. His mind ran with the thought of his friends, his colleagues, teetering down the tunnel, enveloped by darkness, and into the arms of the monsters they so desperately feared.

"Sh-Sh-Shail? You're shivering... you, you are," Mycka said as he stared fearfully at his friend. Shail shook his head and blinked a couple times. His eyes stung as they were rehydrated. He looked down at his palms. They glistened with sweat and shook feverishly. Shail flexed the tense muscles before smearing the sweat onto his dirty pants. They came away with more grit and grim attached.

"Um... So, Gadol went down our tunnel?" said Shail. Mycka nodded and looked uneasily down the passage behind Shail. "And, uh... Rukk is probably in that cavern with Beryl, the Mezmurs, and Gadol?" Mycka's eyes began to water again and he shrunk into a tight ball. "So, we can probably assume that Gadol is being controlled by the Mezmurs since he is the only one who remembers seeing them. Beryl probably saw them too, even though he said he doesn't remember seeing anything. The legends say that they can control minds, which means Beryl could have seen them but they made him forget..."

"S-so, how do we know we haven't seen them? Huh?"

Mycka stared up at Shail with wide, watery eyes.

"I... I suppose we can't know for sure. If they can control whether we know if we've seen them, then anybody in the mine could have seen them and just forgotten... The Dwarves on the surface could have been in contact with them and could be under their control?" said Shail. Mycka sobbed. "But they are only after us because we accidently broke into their burrow..."

He let out a sigh and moved toward Mycka. "We should come up with some sort of plan. I have my pickaxe. But those monsters have yours, and Rukk's, and Gadol's picks. We have a few torches for light, and fire as a weapon. I've got a few rations and one canteen full of water. Do you have anything?" Mycka shook his head while hiding his face in his arms. The terrified Dwarf stayed curled up in the fetal position. Shail sighed and hoisted Mycka up onto wobbly feet. "Come on. Firstly, we need to find the others."

"B-b-but what if the Mezmurs already have them?"

"And what if they are still alive and can be saved?" Shail said, a stubborn look crossing his face. Mycka looked scared, but found the strength to give a meek nod.

"Alright," Shail smiled. "Let's go save the others." He picked up his pickaxe and bag, then handed Mycka his lantern. The two Dwarves crept down the well-known tunnel. As they wandered farther and farther down, Shail realized that the tunnel was getting darker. The only sounds he could hear were the crunching of gravel under his boots and the occasional drip of water. No birds chirped from their tiny cages. Either they had died and decayed on the bottom of their cage or disappeared, cage doors torn off of their hinges, leaving only a couple of brightly coloured feathers. Shail heard Mycka sobbing after they passed the first dead bird.

"Sh-sh-shouldn't we turn back? Doesn't this mean that there's a gas leak or something?"

"Just focus, Mycka, and keep that lantern up so I can see where we are going." As the younger Dwarf lifted the lantern, Shail looked to his right, into pitch darkness. They had walked right in front of the entrance to the cavern without realizing it. Shail gulped. Goosebumps pricked up across his arms.

"So, uhh… we're here, I guess."

CHAPTER 13

Deeper Down

*We explored the caverns today,
further down than we have ever gone before,
or would ever wish to go.*

Shail's nerves were taut across his whole body. He was scared to move. The hairs on the back of his neck stood up. He could feel them watching him from the darkness, silently planning when they would eat him or how they would control him. Slowly, he opened his mouth and whispered, "Rukk?"

Shail half-expected one of the creatures to jump out from the darkness at him. But nothing happened. The darkness stayed still. Mycka waited behind him; his arm holding the lantern shook horribly. Light danced on the cave walls, making shadows waver. The horrors hiding in the dark seemed to appear and disappear all around Shail, only unnerving him more.

"C-come on Mycka! Stop shaking and man up. We're going to go in there and get our friends. But keep a sharp look out, keep quiet, and listen closely. Warn me if you see or hear anything." The lantern's swaying didn't cease. Shail glanced back to see Mycka, wide-eyed and shaking, with tears rolling down his cheeks. Shail squeezed his pickaxe's handle and took one step into the cavern. Gravel crunched under his feet. The sound echoed throughout the space, loud amongst the silence. Slowly, he took another step. Then another. Each time he did, the gravel crunched; and he was sure that everything lurking beyond his lantern's light knew exactly where he was. After a few more steps, Shail reached the edge of his light's beam. He turned around to see Mycka in the same spot, and state, as before.

"Mycka," Shail whispered. He gestured for the younger Dwarf to come closer, but Mycka stayed stuck in his tracks. "Would you rather be left out there, alone in the dark, or be with me, in here, doing something productive?" Mycka shook even harder. Then he looked down at his feet and took one, slow step towards Shail. The gravel crunched; Mycka jumped and ran to Shail's side, into the cavern. Shail put a hand on Mycka's shoulder and gave it a rub before letting go, facing forward, and taking a few more deliberate steps into the darkness.

The two Dwarves wandered through the long, convoluted tunnels that weaved their way deeper and deeper into the mountain. Occasionally, Shail would whisper the name of one of his missing colleagues. He worried that if he yelled there could be a cave-in or the creatures would hear him, but the urge to save the others drove him to still call out. The tunnels here were unlike the ones in the mines. Holes that dripped water were usually plugged overnight, but these ones were slick from condensation as pools of water had collected on the floor. At one point, Shail slipped and tried to brace himself against a rocky wall, but all he got was a handful of slick moss. The tunnels had also been crudely carved. Usually, Dwarves' tunnels were made the same diameter all the way down, but these shifted from the size Shail was used to. At times the Dwarves had to work together to shove or pull one another through the tight walls.

Mycka followed Shail quietly. Shail slowly grew frustrated with Mycka, because the younger Dwarf would jump at the smallest sound or quiver of a shadow and send their only source of light flailing around wildly. At one point, Mycka slipped on the slick ground and almost smashed their lantern.

The longer the two traveled, the more worried Shail grew. He wondered whether they should have gone down a different tunnel. Considering this place was supposed to be the things' den, he had assumed that each tunnel would end after a little while. But this tunnel just kept going on and on. At this point, he was more worried about turning back and not remembering whether they went left or right at certain junctions. He was also amazed that Mycka hadn't questioned him yet, or retreated for fear of the dark. Maybe he knew they were lost now too.

Eventually, after having descended for many miles, the two Dwarves stumbled into a large, open cavernous space. They couldn't tell exactly how big it was, because their light only spread so far, but could judge that the space was large because the walls of the tunnel stretched away from them and their footsteps began to echo a lot more.

"W-wh-where are we?" Mycka whispered after a long pause. Shail jumped and nearly slipped again from surprise.

"Uh... well, I'm not sure, exactly..." Shail whispered back. He suddenly became aware of just how much of a target he and Mycka were. In here, it didn't matter how quiet they were because if anything was in here with them, it would immediately see their light.

Shail raised the pickaxe up to chest height. "Rukk?" he whispered, pausing to allow for an answer. "Gadol?" Pause. "Beryl?" Nothing responded to Shail's calls. "Let's see where we can go from here," Shail whispered to Mycka.

The two eased their way across the right-hand wall of the space. The walls were still covered with moss, but it was drier this time, sort of soft. The comforting, soft, and squishy feeling of the plant life reminded Shail of his warm, welcoming bed back home. Oh, how he missed his mother and father, the warmth of the sun, the smell of fresh air. He had never cherished these pleasures that he had in life before coming down into these dirty, dank, cold mines. Shail began to daydream of what it would be like when he got out of the mines. He longed to quit his job and work in a smithy or the store with his mother. Maybe he could even set up his own mining company, one where the safety of his workers would be put first. This reminded him of why he had wanted to work for Ebony Excavations Inc. so badly. No wonder the benefits were so good. Workers get eaten by monsters down here…

Shail snapped out of the daydream as his hand slid across a sopping wet patch of moss.

"What the…?" He pulled away and stared down at his dirty hand. It was smothered in something red. Shail looked at the wall where his hand had been. The lantern illuminated a large smear of some sort of rust-coloured syrup. "Mycka, what do you make of this?"

The younger Dwarf didn't respond. Shail turned to face him. Mycka's face was blank and stared off to the other side of Shail. "Hey, what is wrong?" Shail followed his gaze. As he turned, he noticed a boot on the ground. It was the same kind that everybody at the mine wore. The toe of the boot was torn, the metal toe guard hanging on by a thread.

"Rukk? Beryl? Gadol?" Shail grabbed Mycka's hand, holding the lantern, and pulled it closer. As the darkness eased further away, the light revealed a pant leg. Shail froze. The material seemed a darker brown than usual. It looked damp. Like something had seeped into the cloth.

Turning around, Shail pried the lantern out of Mycka's stiff fist. Then, he twisted the boy so that he faced the mossy wall and sat him down.

"Just, stay like this, okay? I'll be back in a second." Mycka's teeth chattered but, otherwise, he didn't acknowledge Shail. "Okay," said Shail, nodding. Slowly, he stood up and inched towards the boot. He kept his lantern low and pickaxe high. His eyes darted from the object to the darkness. His nerves were taut from the worry of something jumping out of the dark at him.

CHAPTER 14

Captives

I found them...
But, they couldn't be saved.

Slowly, Shail's light illuminated the boot, then another. Both looked in rough shape. Then the pant leg; it was dark and... flat? Shail kept moving closer. The clothing looked like it had a thin layer of dust. The pants seemed to fill out as Shail moved up to the hips. His light soon touched a shirt. Large tears separated the fabric into loose strands that flayed outward. The light began to shake as Shail quivered. Inside the shreds of fabric, he could see the broken bones of whoever had lived in the clothes. Tears welled up in his eyes. He looked back at Mycka, but the Dwarf was too far away now for the light to touch him. Shail squeezed his eyes shut for a moment, trying to collect the little courage that still resided inside of him. He turned back to the body and took the final step closer to illuminate its face.

A bony skull, stained red in parts, stared back at Shail with empty sockets. He screamed and jumped back. The face disappeared into darkness again. Shail knelt down, resting his pick and lantern on the ground. The skull had the square cheekbones and strong bone structure of a Dwarf. Shail was overcome with grief for the horrible, painful death the man's clothes showed, and for being lost and forgotten among these malevolent caverns. He sobbed for a few moments, sending out a prayer to his god. Then he thought he heard something: a sort of groaning from off in the darkness.

Shail quickly grabbed his pick and raised it to attack. He took quick steps backwards to Mycka. The young Dwarf sat in the fetal position, staring at a blood stain on the mossy wall.

"Sh-should we go see what that is?" Shail whispered to Mycka. The boy did not respond. Shail focussed on the darkness ahead. Another low guttural groan echoed in the darkness. Shail raised his pick, squeezed the handle of his lantern with a shaky fist, and edged closer to the sound.

As he moved further and further away from Mycka, Shail found the corpse of the Dwarf again. This time, he dared not look at it, instead keeping his eyes focussed ahead of him. But, he thought to himself, the corpse seemed to be in a different spot than last he saw it. Glancing back, Shail could only see darkness. It must have just been his mind playing tricks on him.

Slowly and shakily, Shail moved past the body. He continued inching through the darkness. The lantern's light only touched a small area of cave floor around him.

Eventually, Shail found another mossy wall. This one looked even more slick and slimy. Just as he relaxed, thinking he had made it across the cavern without being attacked, Shail heard another moan. This time, he could tell that it wasn't bestial. Something about it just didn't have the sound of a growling animal so much as a man suffering.

"Hello?" Shail whispered into the darkness. No sound came back to him, not even an echo of his own voice. "Hello?" He called out louder. This time, his voice reverberated through the cavern. Another groan responded. Shail took slow, cautious steps, following the cavern wall towards the sound.

After a few steps, Shail began hearing and feeling small fragments of white gravel crunch under his boots. The further he moved across the wall, the more and more gravel he found, and in larger chunks. They took on an odd shape with extraordinarily spiky points, unlike any type of rock Shail was used to seeing.

He plucked one of the fragments off of the ground as he continued walking. It appeared to be very porous, with many bubbles having formed on the inner areas. He wondered what could have made such an odd texture: had it been corroded or was it naturally occurring? Because it had so many holes, the rock was very light. Shail clenched his hand around the piece and found that it broke apart without much effort. As the piece turned to dust, Shail opened his fist and let the particles sift through his fingers.

As the tiny bits of white dust drifted down to the ground, Shail's focus was caught by something under his foot. The toe of his right boot rested on a very large chunk of that white rock. It was round and the outer surface was smooth. As he reached down to grab the rock, Shail lifted his foot off and caused the rock to tip. He jumped back and gasped.

The large white thing he had been standing on was not a rock. It was a skull. Shail's hand began shaking very hard again. The light of his lantern danced around him erratically. His eyes caught glimpses of more large chunks of white bones scattered about the ground: leg bones, spine segments and skull fragments.

Shail screamed and stepped back, tripping on a bone and falling onto his butt. He winced and rubbed his lower back as the pain shot up his spine. As Shail opened an eye, he caught a glimpse of something twitching in the darkness, just out of reach of his light. Shail shakily stood back up and lifted his cracked lantern.

He hesitated for a moment, unsure of whether or not he really wanted to see whatever was lurking in the dark. Finally, he moved one step closer. At first, he didn't realize what he was looking at. It appeared to be another mess of forgotten cloth and bone, with its neck chained to the cave wall. But, then it groaned and twitched its arm. Shail gasped and took another step closer.

"Hello?" Another groan resounded from the sack of skin. Straggles of greasy, thin hair formed a beard. The face resembled a Dwarf's, but it was hard to tell through all of the bloody gashes that maimed the man's decrepit body. A weak murmur escaped his chapped, lightly parted lips.

"H-hey... Um... Are you still alive?" Shail lifted his lantern closer to the man's face. As he did, the man's eyes shot open. Bloodshot green eyes stared. His skeletal jaw dropped open and he let out a furious cackle.

"Hellooooo..." cooed the man's voice once he had calmed down. Shail pulled his lantern back and stood straight, frozen in terror. The man's laughter still echoed through the tunnels.

"Oooh, I remember you... Yes, very, very squishy... They will like that! Oh, yes... they like the squishy ones."

"Th-they? Wait, you know me?" Shail managed to squeak out. Suddenly, he recognized the Dwarf as the man from the train, team 9, who survived the Mezmurs before.

"Yessss," the man licked his lips. "Those nasty little beasties will get you, and then they'll chain you here. But by then, I'll be free. And they'll eat you. Slooooooowly... soooo, sloooowly... yesss. Eventually, you'll be just like me... And then, them..."

"Th-them?" Shail looked around.

"Not the Mezmurs, fool! They are much too powerful to allow somebody like you... or I... to join them. No..." The man lifted a very shaky, weak fist.

"First, you'll be like me..." He extended a finger.

"Then, like that Dwarf you found earlier... no doubt just a bag of bloody bones and rags by now," the man lifted a second finger.

"And then... you'll turn into one of them..." he gestured

at the sea of bones. Shail's teeth began to chatter.

"Oh but you shouldn't worry yet... no... not quite yet. I will be set free long before they ever catch you. Do you know why? Oh... you must know... You must have heard their screams by now. I fell asleep to their screaming not long ago."

"Wait... there are more of you? D-Dwarves chained up?"

"Whaaaat? How have you not seen them? It is rather quiet now... yessss. Maybe they were too hungry. You know... they've been living off of just two of us for the last week or so... Ate our coworkers about a week before that. Seems they need two each week... But there are always more... Ever growing... Always expanding, making more. The more of them, the more of us they need. So, the other two they caught prooooobably aren't enough, no..."

"The other two, where are they?"

"Round this corner. I know so because when they kick and thrash against their chains I can feel the vibrations against my back." He gave a gap-toothed grin. Shail backed up a couple steps from the skeletal figure and ran off.

Could it be Rukk and Beryl? Did they get caught by the Mezmurs?

As he rounded a corner to his left, Shail slipped on a slick spot. "Ouch!" Shail winced and rubbed his back again. His lantern illuminated the liquid that had made Shail slip. Blood... fresh blood. Shail lifted his hands. They were covered in blood too. Tears trickled down Shail's cheeks.

After a moment, he collected himself, slowly stood up, and looked around. On his left, two figures stood, every limb chained to the rocky surface. Large chunks of flesh were missing from their arms and legs. Scratches weaved across the rest of their skin. Their clothes had been ripped from them; all that remained were scraps across their loins. He recognized the bruised and battered faces instantly.

It was Rukk and Beryl. Shail shook even more now and sobbed. One of them groaned and Shail heard the tinkling of metal tapping metal. He looked up. Through his tears he could make out Rukk's eyes. They were open now and stared back, full of terror. Shail gasped.

"Rukk, you're alive! I'm going to get you out of here. Don't worry. We'll break you free and go home and everything will be fine." Shail tried to smile. Rukk started to mumble something, but he was forced into a fit of coughing that ended with him spitting up blood.

"What? Rukk? Are you okay?"

"Run..." Rukk managed to wheeze.

"H-huh?"

"Get outta 'ere," he growled. Shail took a step back and looked around at the expanse of darkness. He could hear a skittering sound now. Distant but audible.

"Go ya id'yot. Run!" Rukk began to have another coughing fit. Shail, shaken, confused, and scared, did as Rukk said. He ran as fast as he could, stumbling and tripping on broken bones. Shail ran towards where he thought he left Mycka. The other, decrepit man's laughter reverberated throughout the cavern. His heart raced and his lantern's light erratically waved throughout the space.

Finally, Shail found Mycka. He was still sitting on the ground but was fingering the mossy wall. His fingers moved the clotted, sticky blood around.

"Mycka..." Shail panted. "We need to go... now!" He

grabbed the younger Dwarf's hand and yanked him up. Shail dragged Mycka across the cavern and back to the passage where they had come in. Glancing back, his lantern reflected blue dots in the darkness. The eyes of beasts, Dyre Rats, or Mezmurs, were watching them. The skittering sounded closer now.

"Come on Mycka! We need to hurry. They're right behind us." The two Dwarves darted through the maze of tunnels, not thinking about the path that they had chosen when coming down earlier. Shail could hear whatever was chasing them. Their claws scraped the tunnel's floor loud enough to create echoes, making it sound like there were hundreds when there was probably half that.

As they turned a sharp corner, Mycka tripped. He fell down onto his hands and knees, letting go of Shail's hand. Shail grabbed the back of Mycka's shirt and tried to hoist the younger Dwarf up, but he felt resistance. Something tugged Mycka away. The material slipped out of Shail's hand. Mycka screamed. Shail grasped at the darkness, trying to catch Mycka's shirt or hand, but his hand just waved through air. Mycka's screams faded away, further and further down the tunnel, back to the cavern.

Shail imagined the young Dwarf chained up where the other Dwarf had been, in a state just as feeble and close to death. He began to cry again. But he knew that if he stayed there, in that tunnel, the Mezmurs would come back and find him, and chain him up, and eat him too. So he ran. Shail ran for a long time, turning corner after corner, not thinking about whether he should go left or right.

Eventually, Shail stopped running. His adrenaline had worn off after not hearing anything chasing him for a while. He was exhausted, dehydrated, and hungry; sad that he couldn't save his friends, but terrified for his own life. Shail didn't want to stay trapped down here, doomed to be controlled by the Mezmurs and feasted upon until they decided to kill him because of new prey. Shaking, he set his lantern down and looked around. Shail had no idea where he was. The tunnel extended into darkness in front of and behind him. A small indent in the cavern created a nook. Shail squeezed his lantern, rucksack, pickaxe and himself in. Then he sat there and picked off chunks of rock to widen the nook. He used these chunks to wall himself in, leaving only a small gap at the bottom of one corner for fresh air to get in.

CHAPTER 15

Last Moments

I'm really happy to have this job,
but, I'm also nervous.
This will be my first time in the mines.

I have no idea how long I've been trapped down here.

Entry #18

To whomever might read this,
otherwise,
Dear Journal,

I think this is it. I've been trapped in this hovel of mine for a few days now. As I write, I am eating my last ration. Yesterday, I finished my water. I'm so thirsty. All I can think about is water. How long will it take me to die without it? Or without food. Which will I die from sooner?

Maybe I'll get lucky and the Mezmurs will get me first. I can hear them in the tunnel, their nails scratching against rock. I can't tell whether they're digging in here or running by.

A couple days ago—at least I think it has been that long—I carved out an air hole between me and the tunnel. It only made me feel more trapped because I can't get out of here. The claustrophobia is killing me. If I leave, they'll grab me, drag me down the tunnel, and chain me up to devour me slowly...

Mycka...

Rukk...

Beryl...

I wonder if that guy from the train, the crazy guy that was chained up, is free yet. I've been thinking about him a lot. I've had a lot of time to think. Sit, starve, sleep, and think. Sit and think... sit and think... Yeah, about that crazy man. When he said free, did he mean that they would let him go? Maybe they would just let me go. Maybe if I left now, they wouldn't care. I could just leave. Go home. And stay there. I should never have left. Never applied for a job. Just stay home, help your mother. I could've done that.

But the man on the train, he said that they brought him back. And he knew. He wasn't crazy. He knew about the Mezmurs. Why the FUCK didn't he tell anybody?! He got away once though… that's what that says. Maybe he can get away again.

Or, maybe "free" meant "dead".

The Mezmurs—

Oh god. Sorry.

They found me.

I can hear Gadol…

He's outside my hole. Oh god. I'm trying to ignore him. Stuffed some shreds of cloth in my ear. No good. No good. He's saying stuff about how they know where I am. He's gonna help them get me out. He's reaching through at me. His arm is too short. Oh thank god. I can hear him… his clunky boots… they're thumping down the tunnel. I can't believe he's still alive. Will they set him free?

I don't know what to do. They'll come for me. They'll kill me. But I can't just leave.

Wait… I hear something.

No, shit, no. Fuck!

They're here. The skittering. Why didn't I just stay home? Oh god. Fuck!

I can't stop myself from shivering. My teeth keep chattering. It's making so much noise. But they know. Gadol told them anyway. So, my making noise doesn't matter. They're going to get me anyway.

Ooooh. I'm so dead.

One of them just reached their arm in here. Theirs are longer. It clawed at my boot. It touched me. Oh god.

I can hear their scratching. It's all I can hear. It echoes in here, underground, in the dark, among the silence. Rocks are shifting, rolling, falling away. I can only imagine all of the gaps in my wall now.

I can feel them staring. They're playing with my mind. It's like they're touching me with their long, bony fingers, playing with my brain. I think I'm going to throw up.

Love

     we love them

        they promise

          keep us safe

             oh

               yes

So

    safe

       down

         here

           with

            them

Oh my god. Fuck. They're playing me. Making me write things? HOW? How is this happening?!
What do I do? Shit. Fuck. What do I do?
I've got my pickaxe. I'll fight them off. Yeah.
I just heard the rocks collapse.
Okay, here it goes.

    Noooo

       Put down

        Do not

          Want to hurt

            Friiiiendsssss

Noooo

Come

     be safe

         love

            become

                one

                    together

The Mezmurs
Mezmurs
Mez
murs

Melissa George,
a Canadian author with a rich interest in the
horror and fantasy genres of films, novels,
video games, tabletop games, and live action
roleplaying games. A graduate of the
University of Toronto: Mississauga with a BA
in English and Professional Writing.
The Mezmurs is her first novel.

Also by Melissa George:

The Act of Constriction
         2016, UTM's *Compass*

Dr. Joseph Workman's Contributions to CAMH
         April 2015, *Friends of the CAMH Archives*
         Semi-Annual Newsletter

How To Make An Ashendael Character
         June 2015, *Underworld LARP Ashendael Forums*

Underworld LARP: Canada's Largest is Expanding Again
         November 2015, The 430th on *Medium.com*

www.ingramcontent.com/pod-product-compliance
Lightning Source LLC
Chambersburg PA
CBHW051259170626
46809CB00004B/1725